D1469915

Quickie Goes to the Big Game

By Donald Driver

Illustrated by Joe Groshek

© 2011 Donald J. Driver

ISBN: 978-0-615-54871-5

Printed in the US by Worzalla. Third Printing January 2012

Anyone who knows Quickie certainly knows how he feels about football. He eats and sleeps it. Football fever was everywhere with pennant-waving fans and chanting cheerleaders. Everyone near and far was preparing for the biggest game, the Dream Bowl.

With the unforgettable playoff loss last year, Quickie could not wait until the playoffs started. Every night before bed, he would pray about going to the playoffs and the Dream Bowl.

Quickie knelt quietly on his knees and prayed: "Dear God, thank you for my family and football. Please let me win the playoffs and one day play in the Dream Bowl. Amen."

Quickie stayed up late knowing he didn't have school the next day. He thought that since there was no school, he could sleep in.
Boy, was he in for a surprise.

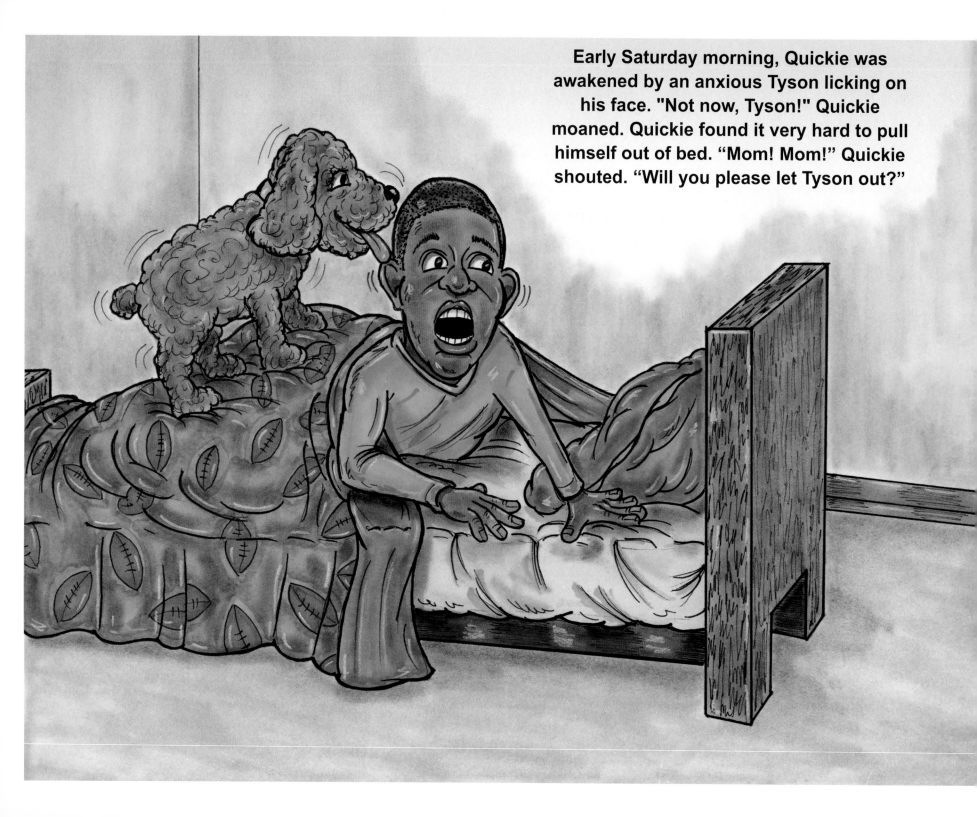

Early Saturday morning, Quickie was awakened by an anxious Tyson licking on his face. "Not now, Tyson!" Quickie moaned. Quickie found it very hard to pull himself out of bed. "Mom! Mom!" Quickie shouted. "Will you please let Tyson out?"

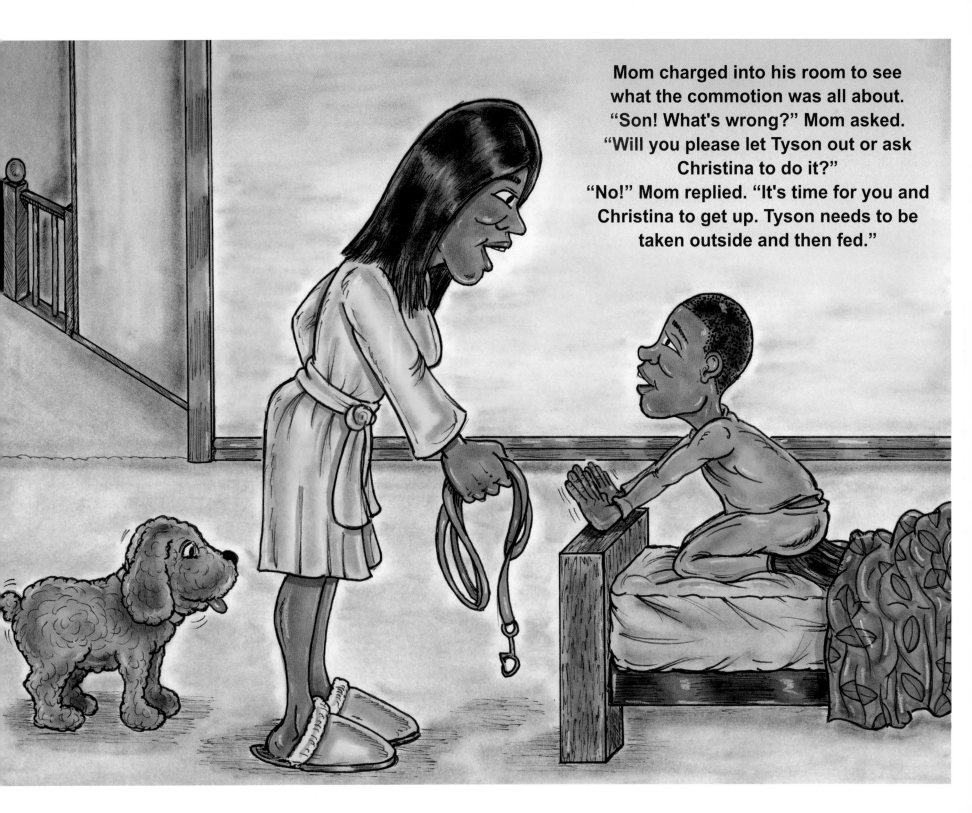

Mom charged into his room to see what the commotion was all about. "Son! What's wrong?" Mom asked. "Will you please let Tyson out or ask Christina to do it?"

"No!" Mom replied. "It's time for you and Christina to get up. Tyson needs to be taken outside and then fed."

Finally dragging himself out of bed with Tyson at his heels, Quickie yelled angrily, "Come on Tyson! If it wasn't for you I could still be sleeping."

Up until now, Quickie's Mom and Dad had been caring for Tyson, but they decided he was now Quickie's and Christina's responsibility. Tyson was more work than Quickie thought he would be. He never knew that his parents had put in so much work caring for Tyson while Quickie and Christina were at school.

Later that afternoon, Quickie was playing football with friends in the backyard when he noticed Tyson was gone. "Hey guys have you seen Tyson?" Quickie asked. "No," one of his friends replied. "Tyson! Tyson!" Quickie shouted over and over again. Quickie ran in the house looking for Tyson.

"Christina! Have you seen Tyson?" Quickie asked. "No! He was outside with you and your friends," Christina said. "Well, he is not out there now. He must have gotten out of the gate," Quickie said. "We must find Tyson before something happens to him and to us," Christina said.

As Quickie and Christina searched the neighborhood from end to end, Quickie remembered Tyson liked to go to the park. "Christina! Let's go to the park." "Why Quickie?" Christina asked. "I think Tyson could be there." "Okay! Let's go," Christina replied.

As Quickie and Christina raced to the park, they saw a blue truck coming down the street. "Hello Dad! How was practice?" Christina mumbled. "Good! Why are you both running down the street?" We are going to the park to play with our friends," Quickie said. "Okay! Be safe and I love you."

"Quickie! You just lied to Dad about going to the park to play with friends. Once he finds out that you lost Tyson and you lied to him, you will be in big trouble," Christina said. "I WILL find Tyson and we WILL still play at the park with our friends. So, I WILL not get in trouble," Quickie replied.

With a long face, Quickie began to cry as he headed home. "What's wrong? Are you crying because Tyson is lost?" Christina asked. "No! Dad is going to be angry at me for lying to him," Quickie said.

As they walked into the house, Dad asked,
"Hey kids. How was the park?"
"Dad! It was bad. I lost Tyson and I lied to you."
"I know Quickie. Tyson ran up to the truck right
after I saw you and your sister."

"What? Tyson is here!" Christina yelled.
"Yes, but you have a lot to learn," Dad said. "Anything worth having, like Tyson, is worth working hard for. It takes much work, but the rewards are great."
It was a lesson Quickie would never forget.

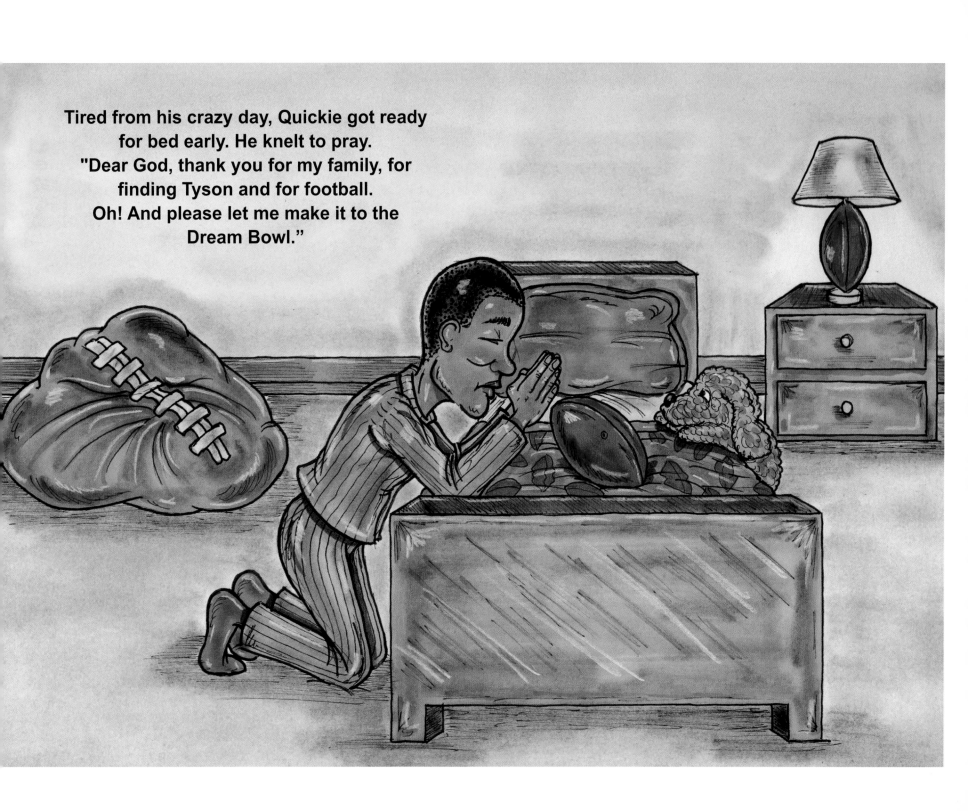

Tired from his crazy day, Quickie got ready
for bed early. He knelt to pray.
"Dear God, thank you for my family, for
finding Tyson and for football.
Oh! And please let me make it to the
Dream Bowl."

As Quickie began to think about football, he got up off his knees and began to move across the room with a burst of energy. "I can't wait until the Dream Bowl," he said looking right at Tyson. He continued to ponder his hopes and dreams about football until he was fast asleep.

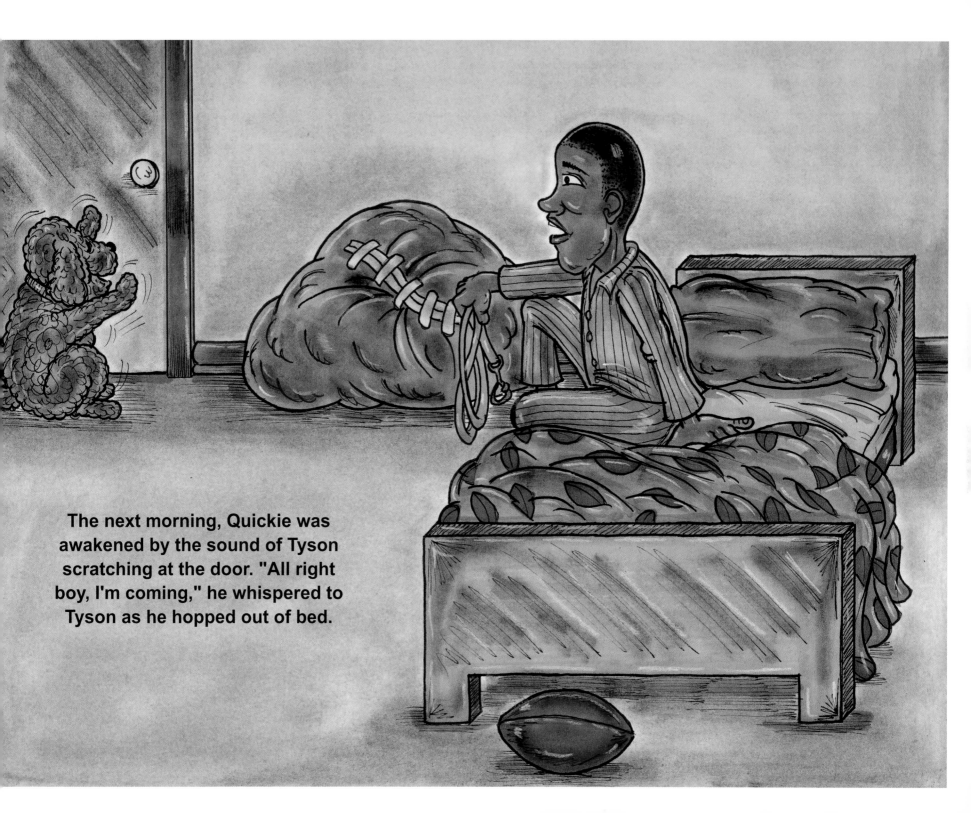

The next morning, Quickie was awakened by the sound of Tyson scratching at the door. "All right boy, I'm coming," he whispered to Tyson as he hopped out of bed.

As the two made their way to the kitchen, Quickie was met by his mother. She was smiling from ear to ear. "I have some great news to share with all of you," said Mom. "What is it?" Christina asked.

2 o'clock! Championship Game! Any football player, young or old, dreams of making it to the Dream Bowl. Quickie was no different and his prayers were answered. "My dad is going to the Dream Bowl!" Quickie yelled. The whole family celebrated that night, but Dad knew that he still had one more game to win.

Two weeks passed and it was time for
the biggest game of Dad's career.
Quickie couldn't believe it, Dream Bowl XLV!
As the family traveled to Dallas,
they could not wait to see Dad.

Christina saw her dad and yelled, "Hey Daddy!"
Dad smiled. "Hello my babies! How was the trip?"
Beaming with pride, Quickie said, "It was great Dad
It's good to be home in Dallas for the Dream Bowl."
Dad said, "I know son. Today will be a big day."

As Quickie was watching the teams play, he was so excited and nervous. Time was moving as slow as a snail. Although Dad's team was ahead, the other team was at fourth down and thirteen yards to go. Down to the final seconds, with one play left, the pass was thrown, but the ball was dropped. Game Over!
Quickie couldn't believe it. He jumped up and down and shouted at the top of his lungs: "We're the Champions!
We won the Dream Bowl!
We really won the Dream Bowl!"

Dream Bowl XLV Champions!!!!!!!!!!!!!!!!!!!!!!!!!!!!!!